AMAZING

PIRATES

Squid Face!

NOT A VERY POLITE WAY to get your attention, I'm afraid, but I need to warn you about what follows. The above is by no means the nastiest name-calling in this sorry collection of tales. When you're dealing with pirates, especially villains as vile as Pugnacious Pete and his criminal crew, you can't afford to be delicate. Pete's awful oaths are only some of the horrors you'll meet.

The first two stories feature three shipwrecks, a dozen dowsings and one definite drowning. After that, things get worse. In the third story, there is horrible torture (by badly played banjo). In the fourth, someone even nastier than Pugnacious Pete turns up. The fifth story has some unholy hypnotism and a mutiny. A psychopathic squid shakes the sixth story. In the seventh, one ship demolishes another. Finally, the last story introduces a character so toe-curlingly callous that you may even feel sorry for Pugnacious Pete.

You have been warned! Read on at your peril . . .

AMAZING

PIRATES

FIENDISH TALES OF DASTARDLY DEEDS

WRITTEN BY NICOLA BAXTER · ILLUSTRATED BY COLIN KING

ARMADILLO

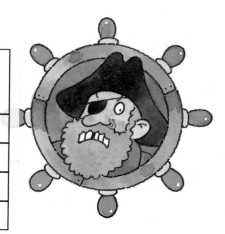

This edition is published by Armadillo, an imprint of Anness Publishing Ltd,
Blaby Road, Wigston, Leicestershire LE18 4SE; info@anness.com

www.annesspublishing.com

If you like the images in this book and would like to investigate using them for publishing,
promotions or advertising, please visit our website www.practicalpictures.com for more information.

Publisher: Joanna Lorenz
Editors: Sally Delaney, Jenny Knight and Elizabeth Young
Designer: Amanda Hawkes
Production Designer: Amy Barton
Production Controller: Don Campaniello

A CIP catalogue record for this book is available from the British Library.

PUBLISHER'S NOTE
The author and publishers have made every effort to ensure that this book is safe
for its intended use, and cannot accept any legal responsibility or liability
for any harm or injury arising from misuse.

Manufacturer: Anness Publishing Ltd,
Blaby Road, Wigston, Leicestershire LE18 4SE, England
For Product Tracking go to: www.annesspublishing.com/tracking
Batch: 6061-20942-1127

Contents

Shipwrecked!

SOMETIMES, watching a stately galleon drifting across the seas, a landlubber may be tempted to think that sailing is a peaceful, calm and restful business. Wrong! And on the *Purple Pimple*, commanded by Pugnacious Pete the Pirate, very, very wrong!

There is creaking (of timbers and Pete's wooden leg) and cursing and clattering and clammering. There are sails that snap and a parrot that squawks. It is not the kind of ship you would choose for a leisurely cruise.

On the particular day when we catch up with Pugnacious Pete and his motley crew, there is an even bigger noise. It goes something like this:

GuUUha SChAM!

No, it's not Pugnacious Pete sneezing or Poisonous Pedro (the parrot) attacking the cabin boy. It's the *Purple Pimple* bashing into an unsuspecting island. For a pirate, Pugnacious Pete's sailing skills leave a lot to be desired. But it will not surprise you to learn that, as he picks himself up off the deck, the mean mariner is not blaming *himself* for the disaster. Suddenly the ship is very empty and the island is very crowded.

"Who," roars Pete, red in the face, "is supposed to be steering this ship?"

Pete's miserable crew knows better than to point out the obvious, which is that Pete himself was at the helm. Poisonous Pedro has no such inhibitions. He squawks the fact loudly into Pete's right ear and then, for good measure, repeats the message in his left ear. Pete's ears haven't seen soap and water for many moons, but that's not the kind of thing that bothers Pedro. His own hygiene would horrify his dear old mother back in Borneo.

Pugnacious Pete pauses only for a second. There's no way he can believe this is his fault. His vile voice rings out once more. "Who," he demands, "is the unfathomable idiot who put this island here?" (Actually, those are not his exact words. I'm having to clean up Pete's language so as not to offend delicate adults – you know what I mean.)

Well, even Pedro doesn't have an answer to that one, so Pete stomps down the gangplank to view the damage.

The *Purple Pimple* could do with a coat of paint. Several repairs are needed. It is not the most beautiful boat on the seven seas. But none of this is because it just collided with an inoffensive island. Amazingly, the collision has done very little damage.

Pugnacious Pete grunts and gurgles a bit, but even he's relieved. There doesn't seem to be much of a problem.

Twenty minutes later, a thought filters through to Pete's brain. "You snivelling shipworms," he says to his crew, "we've got a problem. Can any of you excuses for sailors tell me what it is?"

The sailors try hard not to catch Pete's eye. They all know what the problem is, but no one wants to be the one to say it. Only the cabin boy isn't yet as scared of Pete as he should be.

"We're stuck," he says. "We can't shift the ship."

Pugnacious Pete looks around for something to throw at the cabin boy. That's just the way bad news takes him. As there's not much on the island except a couple of palm trees and a surprised snake or two, Pete looks in vain. In exasperation, he pulls off his wooden leg and smacks the cabin boy smartly around the ears with it – before falling flat on his face.

It's not long before conditions on the island go from bad to worse. There's no fresh water, so the crew is obliged to drink the *Purple Pimple's* rum rations. It doesn't do a bit of good to their brains or their brawn. As the sun goes down, the crew reaches a state of massive marine misery.

"We're all going to die!" booms the bosun in tones of doom.

"First we'll shrivel," sobs the ship's cook, who knows more than he should about death by misadventure.

"I wish I'd been nicer to my poor old mother," moans Pugnacious Pete. "I'll never see her sweet old face again."

In the midst of all this moaning and groaning, the cabin boy is the only person to do something sensible. He shins up one of the paltry palm trees and looks out to sea. Now he shouts, "Ship ahoy!" so loudly that the rest of the crew-members have to cover their ears. The rum has had an unpleasant effect on their eardrums.

But the cabin boy is right. Away on the horizon, a dark ship can just be seen in the gathering dusk.

"Set fire to something. Quick!" shouts Pete. The nearest large thing that would make a good blaze meets his eye and he advances towards it with menace.

A more sensible and sober sailor might have realized that it was not a good idea to set fire to the *Purple Pimple*, but Pete has never been sensible and is certainly not at this moment sober. Luckily, he is quite incapable of lighting a match or making a spark of any kind.

As night slips over the island, the imperilled pirates realize they have no hope of attracting the attention of the passing ship.

The next morning, with throbbing heads and pulsating eyeballs, the pirates spend some hours trying to persuade their brains to open their eyelids. It is therefore not until almost noon that they are able to look around and see that the mystery ship is sailing straight towards them.

"Hooray!" shouts Poisonous Pedro.

"Hooray!" shouts the cabin boy.

"Hooray!" shouts Pugnacious Pete.

Burst Gumboil

"Help!" yell the sailors with one voice. They have spotted the approaching ship's dark sails, its black and white flag, its gleaming guns. It's a pirate ship and not just any old pirate ship. Blackhearted Bill, the nastiest navigator this side of the equator, sails in the *Burst Gumboil*. He is no friend to Pugnacious Pete.

Luckily for the crew of the *Purple Pimple*, Blackhearted Bill is as skilled a sailor as their own clueless captain. With a . . .

SchwAAAAck!

the *Burst Gumboil* sails smack into the *Purple Pimple* and bumps it off the island.

For five furious minutes, confusion reigns. As one crew sails through the air towards a sandy landing, the other crew jumps into the water and swims after the drifting *Pimple*. The *Gumboil* is not drifting. It has become stuck in its turn, and Blackhearted Bill is berating his men as barnacle-bottomed blackguards.

Pugnacious Pete, who has always felt that a sailor's first duty is to stay *out* of the water, is not a great swimmer. Fortunately, his wooden leg floats beautifully and guides him back to his ship. Within a remarkably short time, considering the incompetence of all involved, the *Purple Pimple* is sailing towards the horizon.

Does Pete give a thought to the fate of Blackhearted Bill? Does the image of his dear old mother so much as cross his mind? Does the cabin boy get promotion and an extra ration of weevil-filled bread? If you don't know the answers to those questions by now, you haven't been paying attention. Take a deep breath and plunge straight into the next chapter.

Overboard!

PUGNACIOUS PETE'S best-loved possession – if you don't count his wooden leg – is what he grandly refers to as the Sword of Doom. This perfectly ordinary-looking piece of pirate kit was, according to Pete, wrenched from the grasp of a Spanish prince moments before Pete sent him to a watery grave.

In fact, although it is true that the sword is of Spanish origin, Pete found it in a secondhand shop in the back streets of Cadiz. Nowadays, Pete has told the story of the proud but pathetic prince so often that he believes it himself. What is more, he is positive that the sword has Magical Powers.

Now Pete is as vile a villain as you are ever likely to meet. Just because he is too daft to do any real damage, it doesn't mean that he isn't bad through and through. He thinks nothing of doing a dozen dastardly deeds before breakfast. But Pete also has a silly and superstitious side. He really believes that while the Sword of Doom is in his possession, he will live to darken another day.

The incompetent crew of the *Purple Pimple* can't sail straight at the best of times. When the wind whips around the rigging with a vicious snarl and the sea boils evilly like the cook's so-called soup, this luckless bunch of puny pirates is a disgrace to the seven seas. The ship lurches from wave to wave, while the bosun cowers in an empty barrel, the cook comforts himself with cups of rum, and Pugnacious Pete himself is sick over the side without a thought of who or what is downwind.

At just this moment, as the *Purple Pimple* shudders under the shock of another slosh of sea over its gunwhales, our gallant *(hmmm)* captain cries out in alarm.

"Overboard!"

Up pops the bosun, hopeful that Pete himself may be wallowing in the waves. Up lurches the cook, bothered about the rum barrels. Up pops the cabin boy, hoping to be helpful. They find Pete pointing pitifully at the sea.

"The Sword of Doom!" he cries. "It's gone! Overboard! Give me your dagger; Bosun, you bucket of blubber! Quick!"

As the *Purple Pimple* sways like a blueberry blancmange, Pete starts hacking at the ship's side.

"Stop, Captain!" cries the cabin boy, leaping up. "Don't destroy the *Pimple* and everyone on her!"

Frankly, it would take some time to reduce a galleon the size of the *Purple Pimple* to kindling with only one dented dagger. Pete turns on the youngster with a blood-curdling bellow.

"Blithering bilge-rat! I'm not attacking the boat. I'm marking the spot where the Sword of Doom went over. When this storm stops, we'll know where to dive!"

"D-d-d-dive?" stammers the cabin boy, knowing only too well that Pugnacious Pete has no intention of putting his precious self in peril. "B-b-b-but . . ."

The boy's words are quite literally drowned by a massive wash of water that drenches the deck and everyone on it. When the crew-member rub the salt spray from their eyes, they find they are alone. There is no sign of Pugnacious Pete.

"Captain overboard!" shouts the bosun, clinging to the cook. "And I can't even mark the spot. He's taken my dagger to the deep!"

As the wind howls around them, the ill-fated followers of Pugnacious Pete lean over the side and stare into the stormy waters. Their emotions are, to be honest, mixed.

"It was my best dagger, too!" sniffs the bosun.

"No diving after all!" yells the cabin boy, failing to summon up a look of distress.

"A rum ration to shpare!" slurs the ship's cook.

Several other crew-members begin a hornpipe of celebration before they realize that dancing in a Force Nine Gale is not the brightest of ideas. (But then, if they'd been at all agile in the brainbox department, they wouldn't have sailed with Pugnacious Pete in the first place.)

It is at just this moment that a mighty wave, crashing onto the deck with pirate-pulverizing power, deposits a bedraggled buccaneer in their midst. It is Pugnacious Pete himself, drenched, dazed, but definitely alive.

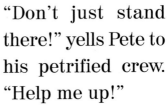

"Don't just stand there!" yells Pete to his petrified crew. "Help me up!"

"Have you still got my dagger?" asks the bosun.

"You didn't find the Sword of Doom, did you?" asks the cabin boy, trying hard to look happy.

"I want to go home!" wails the cook, watching with horror as Pete downs a month's worth of his rum ration to steady his nerves.

Taking care of the captain fully occupies the crew for the next hour or so. It is not until Pete is once more in dry clothes and beginning to feel a little better that everyone notices the storm is over. The *Purple Pimple* is once again drifting gently across agreeably calm seas.

The moment the cabin boy has been dreading has arrived.

"Right," bellows Pete. "Here's a rope. Tie it round your middle, dive down and find the Sword of Doom. Here's the place." Pete points to an ugly notch in the woodwork.

"I'll float!" says the cabin boy, and knows, the moment he says it, that it's a mistake.

"I can soon fix that," growls Pete. He stuffs two cannon-balls into a stocking and ties it around the cabin boy's chest, giving him an extremely odd appearance.

Not surprisingly, the cabin boy is reluctant to leap overboard. Pugnacious Pete offers a friendly hand, or rather, a friendly boot.

Splosh! One small cabin boy and two large cannon-balls hit the water at the same time – and disappear from view with frightening speed.

"What do we do now?" asks the bosun.

"Now," says Pete, chillingly, "we wait."

"I shay," shays (sorry, says) the cook. "Shouldn't someone hold onto that rope?"

It's too late. As the crew watches, open-mouthed, the cabin boy's lifeline slips over the side and disappears under the water. For the second time that day, the crew of the *Purple Pimple* prepares to say farewell; to one of its own. Too soon! With a triumphant shout, the cabin boy's head appears above the water. He is missing one lifeline and two cannon-balls, but against all the odds he triumphantly holds aloft . . . the Sword of Doom!

Pugnacious Pete, overcome by sentiment and rum, claps the cabin boy on the back. The lad is the hero of the hour. In what is perhaps the single most sensible move of his maritime career, the cabin boy decides to say nothing, nothing at all, about the wreck he found directly below the *Purple Pimple*. It contains the wares of one Juan Peseta, supplier of fancy goods to southern Spain (including certain back-street junk shops in Cadiz), who went down with his ship in a storm after unwisely overloading it with swords (of doom, definitely).

Becalmed!

MARINERS MOAN about bad weather. They have a horror of hurricanes. They have a terror of typhoons. I suppose it's understandable. Storms have a habit of upending the most valiant vessel and sending it to the deep. But there is something that pirates hate even more than rough seas – calm seas. Yes, there is nothing worse in a sailor's eyes than being stuck in the doldrums.

One afternoon a couple of weeks before Christmas, Captain Pugnacious Pete and his crew find themselves becalmed in the middle of a very Pacific Ocean. There is no land in sight. All that can be seen, stretching for mile upon nautical mile, is flat, sunny ocean. There are no waves. There is no wind. The sails are as slack as a pair of drawers on a washing line.

"Where are we, Bosun?" asks Pete, gazing at the chart and not at all sure which way up to hold it.

"Two hundred miles south of Barnacle Island, five hundred miles north of Gurgle Point and four hundred miles east of China," says the bosun, confident that Pete hasn't the faintest idea whether he is right or not.

"So what's this?" asks Pete, pointing to a purple patch on the map.

It is, in fact, an . . . er . . . *offering* from Poisonous Pedro after a meal of squid, but the bosun doesn't like to say so.

"It's called Revolting Reef," he grunts, glaring at Pedro. "Trust me. We don't want to go there."

"Are we on course?" asks Pete, suspiciously.

"Absolutely!" says the bosun, which, since he doesn't have the faintest idea where they are headed, is a miracle in itself.

"Then all we have to do is wait," says Pete reasonably. "Cabin Boy, bring me my banjo!"

Now, I believe I've mentioned the natural repugnance a sailor feels for windless weather. Even being becalmed, however, is a billion times better than listening to Pugnacious Pete on the banjo. He only knows one tune, which is something to do with someone being barmy, and he plays it over and over and over again. Very rapidly, it isn't only the person in the song who is barmy. Every member of the ship's company is crawling on the deck and calling for his mother.

Two hours of the banjo later, the crew decides to take desperate measures. They scoop up the glutinous remnants of yesterday's squid stew and stuff it into their ears. (It is, of course, silly to stuff *anything* into your ears *ever*, but you can understand it in the circumstances.)

Now squid stew is not fabulous food but it does have quite wonderful soundproofing qualities. For the rest of the afternoon, the crew-members are blissfully unaware of Pete's playing. They snooze in the sun and wait for the wind to get up.

But the wind, far from getting up, is having the longest lie-in of its life. The afternoon passes. The night passes. Two more long days crawl by. The squid stew smells so bad it has to be washed out of certain loathsome lugholes. Luckily, the sun has stretched the banjo strings. Although Pugnacious Pete is, in fact, playing "Al Barmy" for the three-thousand-and-forty-ninth time, it is no longer recognizable. In any case, even Pete is beginning to tire of it.

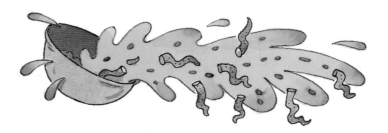

"There must be something we can do," he says. "Hasn't anyone got a pack of cards?"

There is silence. Pete himself ate the cards last time rations were running low.

"I've had an idea," says the cabin boy. "If there's no wind out there to fill the sails, why don't we make some wind ourselves?"

There is silence. Even the unwholesome crew of the *Purple Pimple* thinks this is a gross idea.

The cabin boy turns suddenly scarlet. "I didn't mean *that*!" he protests. "I was thinking, you know, of birthday cakes."

You don't often see a band of nautical ne'er-do-wells thinking of birthday cakes they have known and loved. The bosun sucks his thumb and clutches an imaginary teddy bear. It's the cook who gets the idea.

"You mean like blowing out the candles!" he says. "But will it work?"

"There's only one way to find out," replies Pete briskly. "Come on, all line up in front of the mainsail. Are you ready? Breathe in! One, two, three . . . wait a minute, what are you doing on the sail, Pedro, you pathetic piece of poultry? You're making it twice the weight. Come back here and start flapping your wings or something. Now, are we ready? One . . ."

Pete is surprised to hear several thuds as members of the crew, purple and gasping, literally hit the deck. He has told them to breathe in but not, unfortunately, to breathe out.

Several minutes later, when oxygen levels are back to normal, a second attempt is made.

"Ready, steady, blow!" yells Pete.

None of the crew is at all familiar with Newton's Laws of Motion. In any case, their puny puffing makes no difference. The sail hangs limp. Pretty soon, the pirates are feeling limp, too. Birthday cake candles are one thing. Trying to summon up a Force Nine from a criminal crew close to collapse is something else. Everyone decides to take a rest.

It is at this point that Pete has a truly terrible idea. Terrible for everyone but him, that is. Thoughts of birthday cakes have reminded him of days gone by. And days gone by have brought to mind those Roman galleons powered by hundreds of sweating slaves, chained to their oars.

Pete looks around at his crew and feels depressed. Where are the rippling muscles required? Viewed in that light, the pirates look positively puny. Still, it's worth a try.

The try does not, in fact, last more than a couple of minutes. It soon becomes clear that there are no oars on board long enough to reach the water. The bosun's idea of cutting holes in the side of the ship near the waterline is universally shouted down. Sailors are quite rightly sensitive on the subject of holing their boats. "Water outside, sailors inside!" is their maxim.

Pete's plan to cut down the mast and make it into two giant oars also fails – but only because the saw on board is fit only for removing limbs or scraping barnacles from the bilge.

Then the ship's cook has a bright idea. "What we need," he says, "is an engine! Ships with engines don't need sails."

He is, of course, right. He is also almost two hundred years ahead of his time. If he can only cling to this thought instead of his rum bottle and the *Purple Pimple*, he will be a made man.

He can't, of course. "What?" cry the bosun and the cabin boy.

"Forget it," says the cook quickly. "I'm talking rubbish."

It may be the mention of rubbish, but the bosun decides to come out with some of his own.

"In my experience," he says pompously, "the wind always gets up when you don't want it to. When you're trying to have a picnic, for example. Or . . . or . . . climbing up the mast."

"That's right," says Pete. His eyes fall upon the hapless cabin boy. "Up!" he says. "And make it snappy."

It seems unfair that a boy starting at the bottom in nautical life should be asked to get to the top so rapidly. The cabin boy cowers. Pete reaches for his banjo. The cabin boy climbs. Up, up he goes, until . . .

All of a sudden, a fresh little breeze blows Pete's hat into the rigging and slaps into the sail with a hearty hello.

It's business as usual on the *Purple Pimple*. The sails flap and smack. The timbers creak and groan. Pugnacious Pete smacks. The bosun groans. The ship is speeding along once more, pitching and tossing as only a badly loaded, chronically crewed, atrociously trimmed vessel can.

Pete ponders over the map once more. Pedro adds a few more reefs to the region.

"South by southwest!" says Pete decisively, which just happens to be the way the ship is going anyway.

That night, as a stronger and stronger wind whistles around the *Purple Pimple*'s cabins, Pugnacious Pete and his crew sleep easier in their hammocks, lulled by the sway of the sea. Strangely, all have the same dream. In it, a tiny voice, from somewhere very high and far away, cries, "Help! Help! Help!" over and over again, in tones curiously like those of the cabin boy.

Marooned!

PUGNACIOUS PETE, like most pirates, enjoys telling tall tales, drinking rough rum and musing on the daring and devilish deeds (mostly fictional) he has done. But Pete likes one thing more than any of the above – treasure! At the merest mention of doubloons, Pete goes weak at the knees.

Now there are two main ways for a pirate to get hold of the gleaming stuff. Both involve stealing, of course, but that doesn't matter to mariners with the morals of a shipworm. The first way is to find a big fat ship, laden to the gunwhales with gorgeous gold, and seize it by force. Considerable amounts of killing may be necessary. There is also a serious risk of being killed yourself. Big fat ships tend to have big fat forces on board.

Pete isn't keen on being killed. In fact, he isn't keen on anything that will put him at risk in any way. He has, in the past, been careless to say the least about his body parts (hence the wooden leg), and he dimly realizes that a pirate who loses more than one limb is likely to become an ex-pirate (not to mention an ex-person) pretty soon. So Pete has never vigorously pursued the seizing-ships option.

The other method of treasure retrieval is both easier and more difficult. It involves finding treasure that someone else has seized and hidden, usually on a desert island somewhere. You know the kind of thing – a parchment map and a cross marking the spot. There's often no killing involved and not much chance of getting a dagger in your own gizzard. BUT . . . laying your hands on a decent treasure map these days is not easy.

One blustery afternoon, when the ship's carpenter is bending Pete's ear about the serious state of the *Purple Pimple*'s timbers, an annoying yelling is heard above the slap of the sails and the groaning of the aforementioned timbers. Pete looks round for someone to punch, but there is no one else on deck except the bosun, who is asleep at the wheel.

It takes Pete several minutes to think of looking over the side, and when he does, he is not best pleased by what he sees.

Far below, bouncing on the choppy waves, is an unattractive-looking character in a small open boat. He has no oars and very little else in the way of luggage, food or water.

"Blooming barnacles!" cries Pete. "It's Treacherous Trevor!"

Pete and Trevor go back a long way in the pirating business. Indeed, they both once sailed on the *Adeline Acne*, an ill-fated vessel that met its doom largely because of the combined efforts of Pete and Trev to save it. However, more recent events, not unconnected with Pete's lack of limb, began a deadly emnity between the pirate pair. Pete and Trev have not exchanged a civil word for ten years.

Despite his perilous situation, Treacherous Trevor is not about to start now.

"Let me on board, you scummy excuse for a seaman!" shrieks Trevor.

"Not in a million years!" growls Pete. "And not tomorrow either!"

A look of low cunning comes over Trevor's foul face. "I've got something in-ter-est-ing here!" he chants in a singsong voice.

Pete is disgusted but he can't help himself. "What is it, wormbrain?" he charmingly enquires.

Then Treacherous Trevor waves what looks very much like . . . surely not! Yes, it is something resembling a treasure map!

Trevor's Treasure Map
P.t.o.

There follows one of those you-throw-it-up-first-no-take-me-on-board-first conversations that can go on and on. Frankly, life is too short to trouble ourselves with that. All you need to know is that four hours later (I told you they can go on and on), Pete and Trev are sitting down at the captain's table and peering at the map.

Neither of the two nefarious ne'er-do-wells wants to let anyone else in on the secret, so it takes them a terribly long time to locate the treasure island an Pete's sea charts. Even then, it's hard to be sure they have the right one. Luckily, it's not far away.

"Here's the plan," says Pete. "You and I will land on the island and find the treasure. Then we'll bring it back on board when it's dark and share it out. The rest of the crew need never know anything about it."

"Good idea," says Trevor sweetly.

If this polite exchange makes you suspicious, you're dead right.

My plan for you, squid features, is that you get left on the island and I sail off with the treasure.

Share it out? The only thing I'll be sharing is the toe of my boot when you're climbing back onto the ship. Then it's "Hasta la vista, pug face!"

That afternoon, Pugnacious Pete can be heard casually telling the bosun to anchor by a small, faintly familiar island and to break out the rum for the entire crew. The bosun can hardly believe his ears. But Pete's plan, for once, works like a dream. By the middle of the afternoon, no one is in any state to notice two greedy gold-seekers creeping down the gangplank and onto the shore.

"Which way now?" hisses Pete, for Treacherous Trevor has the map.

"This way!" squeals Trevor, plunging into the undergrowth. Within thirty seconds, Pete is alone, lost . . . and livid.

Pugnacious Pete settles down under a palm tree by the shore. He tries hard not to think about treasure. He tries harder not to think about Treacherous Trevor. He tries hardest of all not to think about Treacherous Trevor creeping ever closer to some perfectly good treasure that should by rights (well, by wrongs) belong to only one person – Pugnacious Pete himself.

Pugnacious Pete doesn't find thinking easy. He finds not thinking even more difficult. Just when his brain has reached a degree or two below boiling point, it suddenly has another thing to worry about.

Boink!

Something very large and very hard hits Pugnacious Pete's heated headpiece.

Meanwhile, in a cave not a million miles away, Treacherous
Trevor is puzzling over his treasure map. He feels sure that it will
lead him to a chest positively overflowing with florins, drowning
in doubloons, piled high with pieces of eight – if only he can work
out which way up to hold it.

In the brains department, Treacherous Trevor is only slightly less
challenged than Pugnacious Pete. He creeps out of the cave with
a dim thought that he can find out which way is up by looking at
the sun and his watch. It is a pity that
he doesn't actually have a watch. He also hasn't
considered that while he has been pondering
over his parchment, night has fallen.

Suddenly, Trevor doesn't feel terribly happy about being in the dark on an unknown island. Without trying very hard at all, he can hear a horrible screeching from his left, a disturbing howling from his right, and a deeply worrying slithering sound from somewhere near his bare toes. Trevor – for the very first time in his life – begins to wish that Pugnacious Pete is by his side.

A second later, all thoughts of Pete fly out of Trevor's brain as he hears the grunting and screeching of a monstrous beast crashing through the undergrowth. It sounds like a dozen rhinos rushing to the attack. Whimpering, Trevor turns to flee back into his cave, but in the dark, he can no longer see it. Instead, he runs smack into a palm tree and clings to its trunk, making pathetic sounds and shivering like a jellyfish.

The beast is bellowing. It is thrashing through the trees. It is only inches away. It smells ghastly. It is . . . Pete!

As the moon struggles through the straggly clouds, Trevor and Pete recover from the shock of their collision. In a surprisingly short time, Pete's pounding and pudding-sharp mind is back on the business in hand.

"Did you find it?" he hisses.

"Find what?" asks Trevor, attempting a casual whistle.

Pete takes him by the collar and demands to see the map.

"The m-m-m-map?" asks Trevor, holding up his empty hands. Clearly, the map has been dropped somewhere in the trampled undergrowth. Equally clearly (or rather, equally unclearly), moonlight is inadequate lighting for a fingertip search.

"There are lanterns on the *Pimple*," yells Pete. "Come on!"

But there is a problem in leaving a ship in the charge of a bosun too drunk to notice if his captain is present. Sometimes, just sometimes, such a bosun might take it into his head to set sail . . .

Swashbuckled!

WATCHING IN DISBELIEF as the *Purple Pimple* sails erratically away, even Treacherous Trevor and Pugnacious Pete, two seasoned sea-dogs, run out of salty language. The last oath dies away, and the full horror of the situation strikes both pirates. It is bad enough to be marooned on a small island alone. It is almost unbearable to be there in the presence of a truly obnoxious character – and as far as obnoxiousness goes, there isn't much to choose between Trev and Pete.

After spending a most uncomfortable night up a palm tree (for fear of wild animals below), Pete and Trev breakfast with little enthusiasm on coconuts and clams. The thought of this diet for weeks, months or . . . perish the thought . . . years adds another layer of gloom to an already overcast day.

Trawling about in his mind for something more cheerful to think about, Pete suddenly remembers the treasure . . . and the missing map. The same thought occurs at the same moment to his breakfast companion.

"Think I'll just go for a stroll," says Pete casually.

"Good idea. I'll come too," says Trevor, not deceived for a moment. But despite hours of aimless strolling in the general vicinity of the cave, no map can be seen. Pete and Trev sit down in shared despair.

"Maybe your crew will come back," says Trev, hopefully.

Pete snorts. He knows only too well the navigational ability of his men. The chance of them finding a small island in a very large ocean is tiny. Worse, they may not even want to! Pete regrets a number of cutting comments, peculiar punishments and weevil-infested meals he has doled out on the *Pimple* in the past.

Only two things keep the pirates together. One is Trevor's clam-opening penknife. The other is Pete's coconut-attracting head.

Whenever he sits down under a palm tree, a ripe coconut skitters across his skull. It saves a lot of climbing. A diet of clams and coconut is bad enough, but a diet of only clams or only coconuts is unthinkable. Somehow or other, the pirates manage not to strangle each other as the days pass.

Here's another point where we should skip forward a bit. I can tell you briefly that nothing at all exciting happens on the island for the best part of fourteen months. Beards and hair grow. The clam population decreases. That's it. We will fast-forward to a morning when the sky is blue, the sun is sparkling on the dancing waves, and a set of white sails is seen on the horizon.

As soon as Pete spots the sails, he and his companion begin running up and down the beach waving their arms. When this doesn't seem to have any effect, they strip off their ragged clothes (avert your eyes if you need to) and wave those instead. Clothed, these pirates are not wholesome. Unclothed, they are a sight that any self-respecting ship would flee from. Strangely enough, the unknown craft comes gradually closer.

As the galleon drops anchor in the bay, Treacherous Trevor and Pugnacious Pete peer at it with increasing amazement. Its sails could advertise washing powder. Their gleam is almost too much for Pete, who is forced to swap his eyepatch to the other eye (he only wears it for effect). Every timber of the ship is smooth and clean. There isn't a barnacle or a trace of a passing seagull anywhere. On deck, sheets (ropes to you and me) are neatly coiled. Some respectable washing flies from the mast.

"You don't think . . ." Pete begins.

"It couldn't b-b-be!" stammers Trevor.

But it is. "Perfect Peregrine!" groan the pongy pirates.

"Ahoy there, chaps!" comes a cheery voice, and Perfect Perry wades ashore. As usual, he looks impossibly handsome. His teeth glint as he smiles. His cuffs are crisp. His curls are crisper. His blue eyes positively twinkle.

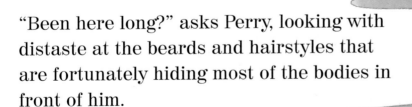

"Been here long?" asks Perry, looking with distaste at the beards and hairstyles that are fortunately hiding most of the bodies in front of him.

"Not long," replies Pete carelessly. "Might stay on a bit, actually. Very pleasant climate. Very fine clams."

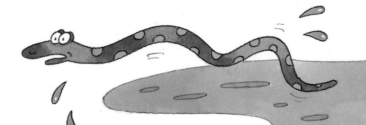

One of the most annoying things about Perfect Peregrine, apart from his mission to rid the sea of pirates, is that he is as clever as he is clean. He understands in a flash that there is more to the situation than meets the eye.

"So what brought you here?" he enquires genially. "Wildlife? Holiday? Treasure?"

Pete and Trev are hardened pirates. They are used to looking mean and deeply inscrutable. But frankly, after fourteen months, they are totally out of practice. At the mention of treasure, they twitch.

"Got a map?" asks Perfect Perry with a gleam in his eye. It is costly to keep a galleon as ship-shape as the trim *Maiden's Blush*.

"No," says Pete.

"Yes," says Trev, at the same moment. "I mean, no."

Perfect Perry never resorts to the types of torture with which Pugnacious Pete is familiar. The thumbscrews and the toetwisters are distasteful to him. But he makes up for a lack of ironware with more than his share of cunning.

"Fancy a bit of lamb stew?" he asks. "Cherry pie? Strawberry shortcake? Barrel of rum . . . purely medicinal, of course. Or maybe you'd rather carry on with the clams. Quite understand. Delicious shellfish."

He hasn't even finished speaking before Pete and Trev, visibly drooling, are clutching at his knees and begging to be taken on board the *Maiden's Blush*.

"All in good time, chaps," says Peregrine. "Let's have a little chat about maps first."

When Peregrine hears that the map has been lost, his smile and his charm both become a little chilly. Then he probes further.

"But you looked at the map pretty carefully?" he asks.

"Yes, but we don't remember," says Pete gruffly.

Perfect Perry appears cheered by this news. "Of course you don't," he replies soothingly. "Now come on board and have . . . well, a bath would be a good start, I think."

That evening, blissfully full of lamb stew and strawberry shortcake, and cleaner than he has been since his mother last excavated his ears, Pete swings gently in a hammock while the ship's boy plays soulful ditties on the mandolin. Pete wonders

whether to jump up and ask if there's a banjo on board, but he decides against it. And, just as he begins to feel sleepy, he hears a somewhat familiar voice in his ear.

"You are beginning to feel sleepy," it says with uncanny accuracy. "You are beginning to feel very, very sleepy."

Pete closes his eyes. The voice drones on.

"You are fast asleep. You are thinking back to the last treasure map you examined. You are seeing it in your mind's eye. You are taking this pencil and copying it onto this paper. You are drawing very carefully and not going over the edge. You are not even thinking about chewing the very fine pencil. You are finishing your drawing. You are handing it over . . . and the very fine pencil. You are sitting up in your sleep. You are walking across the deck. How beautiful the water looks. How inviting. What a lovely moment for a swim. . ."

It is the squawking of Poisonous Pedro that brings Pete to his senses. It is the digging of Poisonous Pedro's claws into Perfect Peregrine's scalp that causes the howling. It is the sight of Perfect Peregrine's pristine hairpiece gliding through the air that persuades his crew to join with Pete and Treacherous Trevor in a most satisfying mutiny.

After all, clean living and deck-swabbing can only hold a crew's interest for so long. After a while, any self-respecting seaman wants to give up baths and swear a bit. As Perfect Peregrine performs a perfect breaststroke towards the island so recently home to Trev and Pete, the crew gives a hearty cheer for its new captains and sets sail for the Spanish Main, while Poisonous Pedro sets about giving the spotless sails a little more of a lived-in look.

Suckered!

IT IS REMARKABLE how quickly standards on a well-ordered ship can sink. Within hours of the arrival of Pugnacious Pete and Treacherous Trevor, there are weevils in the bread and the lamb stew has acquired that strange, slimy consistency so familiar from the *Purple Pimple*.

To Pete and Trev it feels like home, although Pete does still think fondly of his old Pimple and wonders what wide ocean she is sailing now. He also has plans of deep and dark revenge against the bosun, should he ever come across that scurvy seaman again.

There are, of course, things about the *Maiden's Blush* (or the *Maiden's Rash* as she soon comes to be known) that Pete finds strange. For a start, he has a helmsman who can read a chart. For the first time in his life, Pete has half an idea of where he is going. He's not sure he likes this. It takes the sense of adventure out of pirating somehow.

Secondly, Pete has a co-captain. He is absolutely certain he doesn't like that! In fact, Treacherous Trevor is becoming more annoying every day – and more treacherous, too. It's not long before both captains spend all their time plotting against each other. It is only because they are quite hopeless at planning that both are still on board.

At night, the captains sleep in hammocks in the captain's cabin. Pete has been careful to position himself over a particularly creaky floorboard, so that he has warning if anyone happens to come creeping up. He is also, in case the worst comes to the worst, near a Pete-sized hatch. A dip in the ocean is better than a dagger in the ribs, he thinks.

One dark, sultry night; Pete and Trevor are swaying gently in their hammocks. As usual, each has one eye open, although Pete has chosen to open the eye under his eyepatch, which makes him believe the night is particularly dark.

When Pete feels something clammy curling its way around his neck, his first thought is that Trevor is up to his old tricks.

"Oh no, you don't!" he cries, and sinks his teeth into Trevor's arm. He can't help noticing two significant things. Trev doesn't shout out. His arm is strangely rubbery.

Then a second arm wraps itself with astonishing strength around Pete's knees. Pete is beginning to panic when a third arm begins to squeeze him around his rather large middle.

Now even Pete, not famous for his thinking skills, knows that Treacherous Trevor only has two arms.

As Pete writhes in the grip of his assailant, his eyepatch falls off. A shaft of moonlight shines through the cabin. On the other side, Treacherous Trevor's eyes are bulging as one massive suckered arm squeezes his face. Three suspiciously similar suckered arms are hugging Pete in a far from affectionate way.

Suddenly, the *Maiden's Rash* seems to leap in the water. Pete, deposited rather quickly on his head on the floor, doesn't notice for a moment that the deadly grip has ceased. He is more aware of the fact that Trev's toe is wedged up his (Pete's) nose.

A few minutes of confusion, cursing and toe-removal follow, during which the *Maiden's Rash* is violently shaken (actually, this helps with the toe-removal). When Pete and Trev at last scramble out on deck, the sight that meets their eyes as dawn glimmers on the horizon is gruesome indeed.

The ship is in the grip of a squid so huge that it is waving the *Maiden's Rash* about like a toy. Pete can hear the crew rattling about below. Clinging on for dear life, he and Trev have an urgent council of war.

"I suggest we hack off its arms," says Pete, clutching the Sword of Doom.

"There are dozens of them!" gasps Trevor. Counting is not his strong point. "There are harpoons in the hold."

Pete hasn't the faintest idea how to throw a harpoon. It sounds dangerous and difficult. Besides, he is beginning to think there is a fatal flaw in all these plans.

"We might just make it cross," he yells. "Well, crosser. What if it decides to dive? Maybe we should try being nice to it!"

Neither of the pirates has any idea of how to set about being nice to a squid. Finally, Trev has a thought and heads for the galley. Surely a well-fed squid is a happy squid?

Working on the same lines, Pete looks around for his old banjo. Soothing music, he thinks, might calm the beast. Of course, Pete's banjo is still on board the *Purple Pimple*, but there is a mandolin.

Pete lashes himself to the mast so that he has two hands free. Trev, meanwhile, is filling the cannon with leftover lamb stew (now several weeks old) and preparing to fire in the general direction of what he takes to be the squid's mouth.

Pete's banjo playing is poor. His efforts on the mandolin are worse. Within two seconds, the unsuspecting squid is assailed by Pete's version of "What Shall We Do With the Drunken Sailor?" (played at half speed in the wrong key) and a faceful of smelly stew. It does not hesitate. The *Maiden's Rash* is dumped unceremoniously back in the water, and the squid heads at top speed for the peace of the deep.

"I knew my playing would work," says Pete, struggling to free himself from the mast.

"What do you mean? It was me feeding it that did it!" shouts Trev. "That's typical of you . . ."

And so, to the happy sound of captains complaining, the *Maiden's Rash* sails on towards adventures new.

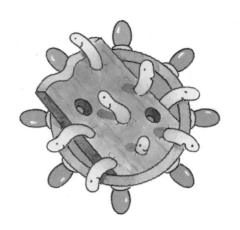

Timber!

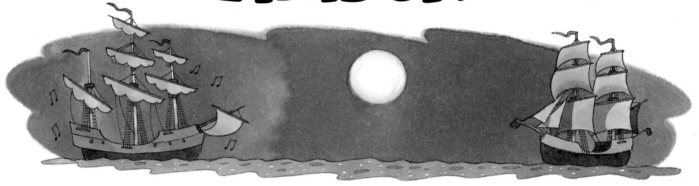

T HE OCEANS OF THE WORLD are wide. They are, in fact, twice as wide as the lands of the world, on which millions of human beings trudge up and down daily. By comparison, the traffic on the wide, blue, wet stuff is tiny. It should be well nigh impossible for two vessels with a vast ocean between them to collide. You can guess what is coming . . .

Late one night, when Pete and Trev are, as usual, hovering delicately between sleep and suspicion, a skull-shattering shock hurls them both from their hammocks. This time, it is Pete's bottom that bears the brunt of the impact, while Trev ricochets around the walls before coming to rest in the hammock he has recently left.

Pete's first confused thought is of squid. You will understand why. His second is that Treacherous Trevor is up to his old tricks. He doesn't get as far as a third thought because it is at this moment that the painfulness of his posterior truly strikes him.

"Owwwww!" yells Pete.

"Whaafnaafnum?" demands Trevor, his voice muffled by the hammock, which has spun around and made him into a kind of sea-going sausage.

"H-e-l-p!" comes a pitiful voice from far below, followed by other pitiful voices sending much the same message.

Pete staggers on deck and peers through the gloom. There is something strangely familiar about the shouting and splashing surrounding the ship.

Just then, a beam of moonlight struggles through the ragged clouds. Pete gasps. He thinks of his bruised bottom and gasps again, But really, his first gasp was the most important one. All around, the sea looks like soup. That is, it looks like watery stuff with bits floating in it – which is what soup is, really.

On closer inspection, there appear to be two kinds of bits. Most are bits of wood. In fact, bits of wood that look suspiciously as if they have once been bits of ship. Pete looks around in alarm, but there are no disturbing glugging sounds coming from the *Maiden's Rash*. She has all her important parts and does not seem to be about to sink into the said soup.

The other floating bits also resemble chunks of wood but are, in fact, people. And not just any people. These are very familiar people indeed.

"Captain!" yells one of them. "Captain, my dear old darling! Come and have a swim. It's lovely once you're in!"

"Bosun!" Pugnacious Pete can hardly believe his eyes. There is his errant second-in-command, apparently as much under the influence as ever. But if that is the bosun, where is the *Purple Pimple?*

Suddenly, Pete's heart seems as bruised as his bottom. Even pirates have feelings. All around him, scattered on the waves, are the remains of his beloved flagship. The *Pimple* is no more.

Much later, as the sun rises over the *Maiden's Rash*, Pete's sadness turns, predictably enough, to fury. The crew of the *Purple Pimple* is dripping dismally on the deck. Only the bosun, for obvious reasons, is still resolutely cheerful.

"What have you done to my ship, you blithering blister on a barnacle?" yells Pete, gesturing wildly at the waves, where pathetic remnants of the aforementioned vessel are still bobbing bravely.

"We were run into," says the bosun, speaking very distinctly but not very tactfully, "by a big fat tub called the . . . er . . . the *Measle*, or something like that."

"You were not run into, herring head!" shouts Pete. "We were run into! Why couldn't you look where you were going? You've destroyed a perfectly . . . perfectly . . . fine friend . . ." There is a catch in Pete's pugnacious voice.

"It wasn't perfectly fine, you know." The ship's carpenter decides to add a word. "Those worms were past dealing with. The tiniest tap could have burst the *Pimple*. I often told the bosun so."

"And we were sailing under desperate difficulties," the bosun goes on blithely, "after you jumped ship, Captain . . ."

"Jumped ship!" Pugnacious Pete becomes purple with rage. "I did not jump ship! I merely . . . er . . . went ashore for a bit. When I came back, you were gone! Jumped ship, indeed! The only person doing any jumping here, you whelk-brained sea slug, will be you. Walking the plank always seemed a silly idea to me, when a swift swish with the Sword of Doom could do the job, but it's beginning to look attractive. At noon today, Bosun, you'll be taking your final constitutional."

As the sun continues to climb the sky, and the effects of the night before begin to wear off, the bosun starts to understand the seriousness of his situation. He cudgels his brains for a way to get around his old captain.

He might have succeeded, too, if it hadn't been for Treacherous Trevor. When finally released from his hammock, Trev is peevish to say the least. He has missed all the fun of the rescues. He has missed seeing Pete turn purple. The only bit of fun remaining, as far as he can see, is the prospect of the bosun walking the plank.

Pete, of course, is anxious not to look soft in front of Trev. So when the bosun returns first Pete's treasured eyepatch and then Pete's beloved banjo, the co-captain hardens his heart against his erstwhile number two.

"It's time," he says at last. "Now, who's got the plank?"

There is no suitable plank on board the *Maiden's Rash*, so the crew fish a suitable bit of the *Purple Pimple* out of the sea and set it up on deck, nailing it down at one end but letting it wobble dangerously at the other, where it overhangs the sea.

The carpenter from the *Purple Pimple* seems strangely excited by all this. At least, he keeps jumping up and down and trying to attract Pete's attention. Pete ignores him.

"Come here, scum bucket," he invites the bosun, with his usual irresistible charm.

The bosun tries joking. He tries pleading. He tries getting down on his knees and weeping. Pete is not impressed. Waving the Sword of Doom carelessly near to the bosun's nose, Pete urges the sobbing seaman onto the plank.

"Now, walk, you sliver of squid slime!" yells Pete.

The bosun tries. He really does. But his knobbly knees are knocking together so ferociously that he can barely put one foot in front of the other. When he reaches the middle of the plank, he stops.

Pete has had enough. With a roar, he charges onto the plank, swiping wildly with the Sword of Doom. Taunting and tickling with its tip, he urges the bosun towards the very end of the plank.

The plank sways. The bosun totters. Pete, holding out the famous blade, is better balanced, but even he turns a little green around the gills. Back on deck, the ship's carpenter begins to make little squeaking noises.

And then . . .

Craa-a-aaa-aaa-eeee-aaaak!

The plank snaps in half and into the sulky sea tumble the bosun, Pugnacious Pete and several hundred shipworms who were wiggling their way out of the plank.

"I tried to tell him," cries the ship's carpenter, running to the side.

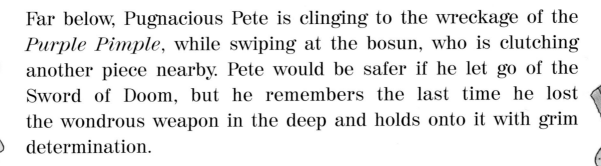

Far below, Pugnacious Pete is clinging to the wreckage of the *Purple Pimple*, while swiping at the bosun, who is clutching another piece nearby. Pete would be safer if he let go of the Sword of Doom, but he remembers the last time he lost the wondrous weapon in the deep and holds onto it with grim determination.

"Do something!" yells Pete to the watchers high above on the *Maiden's Rash*. They do. They laugh.

Treacherous Trevor finds that he has not, after all, missed the chance to see Pete at his most purple. But the bosun realizes that his chance has come to redeem himself. Carefully avoiding the swinging Sword of Doom, he drags Pugnacious Pete to the side of the ship, where the cabin boy has thoughtfully let down a ladder.

Later that night, as he looks around at so many familiar faces, Pete reflects that the *Maiden's Rash* is looking and feeling more and more like the much-lamented *Purple Pimple*.

And, far below, several worms from the Pimple begin the happy task of chomping their way through the trusty timbers of the *Maiden*. It's an ill wind . . .

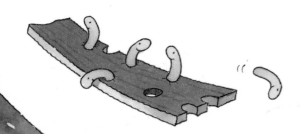

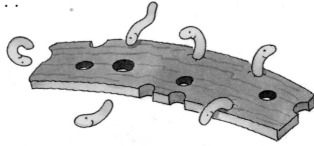

Scuppered!

LIFE ON THE OCEAN WAVE is rarely comfortable and frequently dangerous. Pugnacious Pete has always, so to speak, sailed pretty close to the wind, but recently even he has begun to think that things are a little *too* exciting on board the *Maiden's Rash*. Even if you don't count psychopathic squid and mid-ocean collisions, there is the perennial problem of Treacherous Trevor.

For Trevor certainly is treacherous – and not in a nice way. In recent weeks, Pete has found Dutch Death Fish in his spare underpants, broken glass in his boots, and Cantonese Killer Crabs in his hammock. He has also seen Trev muttering with various members of the combined crew of the *Rash* and the *Pimple*. The word "mutiny" strolls in a sinister way through the darkest comers of Pete's mind.

As Pete becomes increasingly ill at ease, the crew, too, gets edgier. Soon, everyone is creeping around, constantly looking over their shoulders and jumping at the creak of a plank or the squawk of a parrot. Of course, they are bumping into each other a lot, too. (It's the looking over the shoulder that does it. You really need wing mirrors if you are going to go in for a lot of that sort of thing.)

One afternoon, when dark storm clouds are billowing above the *Maiden's Rash*, and a deep sense of foreboding is swirling around the topsail, a ship is sighted on the horizon.

"A sail! A sail!" cries the cabin boy, wriggling in the rigging.

"Aha!" cries Pete, leaping to his feet. He has been sitting on the deck, a pistol in one hand and the Sword of Doom in the other, wishing he had a better idea of Treacherous Trevor's precise whereabouts at that moment.

Now, the possibility of some action at last-against an unknown enemy instead of an only-too-familiar one-stirs Pete's blood. Who knows what may be on the fast-approaching ship? Gold? Jewels? Chocolate cake? Pete lets out a bloodthirsty yell.

"Yo ho ho! What manner of ship is she?" he asks the cabin boy.

Thwack! The luckless cabin boy lands suddenly at Pete's feet. Well, foot. His face is white. His lips are trembling. His fingers are quivering. And not all of this is due to the fact that he has landed on one of the Cantonese Killer Crabs.

"What is it, boy?" yells Pete, impatient for news.

The cabin boy twitches. "It's D-D-D-D-D . . . !" he tries.

"Dutch? Danish? Drifting? Dusty? asks Pete.

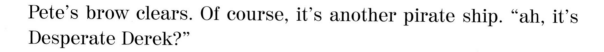

"No! It's D-D-D-D-D . . . !" There is a look of agony on the cabin boy's face. (The Killer Crab isn't looking too healthy either.)

Pete's brow clears. Of course, it's another pirate ship. "ah, it's Desperate Derek?"

"No! D-D-D-D-D . . . !"

Other crew members join in the game. "Dark-hearted Dave? Dire Dominic? Dastardly Donald?"

As the cabin boy struggles to reply, the strange ship has been gaining on the *Maiden's Rash*. It's as evil a craft as you will ever see. As Pete, Trev and their crew look up at last, the awful truth dawns on them. It is much, much worse than Dark-hearted Dave, Dire Dominic, or Dastardly Donald. With one voice, they gasp . . .

"Dreadful Doris!" and they turn to look at Pugnacious Pete, who is making a desperate attempt to throw himself overboard.

"Oh no, you don't!" says Treacherous Trevor, grabbing his co-captain without ceremony. "This I have to see!"

Quaking, Pugnacious Pete is dragged across the deck. At the same moment, the captain of the approaching ship, named, as is now clear, the *Athlete's Itch*, leaps lithely on board the *Rash*. It is Dreadful Doris herself, the meanest, baddest, fiercest pirate the world has ever known.

"Hello, Pete, you miserable maggot," she cries, in a voice that could stop a tornado in its tracks.

"Hello, Mum", mutters Pete.

There are words that are rarely said and even more rarely written, but I am going to write them now . . . poor old Pete. He may be bad. He may be ugly. He may be unhygienic. But no one deserves a mother like Dreadful Doris. She has a voice like a foghorn. She lives to harass and humiliate. She dresses in a way that would make any son shudder. She has terrible taste in earrings. And she is completely unaware of any of these failings.

Pete looks with panic at his crew. To a man, they turn away and begin whistling. There is no choice. Pete stumbles forward to be embraced by the woman whose perfume is the only known cure for an infestation of shipworms.

Poor old Pete. He sits on the deck with his mother, while she reminisces in a voice that reaches the top of the topsail and the bottom of the bilge. She leaves nothing out. Pete's potty training. Pete's lack of success with girls. Pete's personal hygiene problems. Pete is well and truly scuppered.

And now, Doris declares, she will invite the crew of the *Maiden's Rash* to a special supper on board the *Athlete's Itch* – that is if Pete's sensitive stomach is up to it.

Pete shuts his eyes and prays for the arrival of a giant squid.

That night, on board the *Athlete's Itch*, Pete endures tortures that are too painful for me to mention. Suffice it to say that the evening begins with Dreadful Doris showing Pete's baby pictures and gets worse. Poor Pete can't even drown his sorrows in rum, for the eagle eye of his mother glitters alarmingly if he so much as toys with a tankard.

Of course, everyone else enjoys the evening enormously, and none more so than Treacherous Trevor. Nothing in the world delights him so much as to see Pugnacious Pete in agony. Dutch Death Fish and Cantonese Killer Crabs cannot do half the damage of a mother in full flood.

It is very late when an all-too-sober Pete staggers to his hammock at last. He doesn't even bother to check it for broken glass or sea snakes. Blessed oblivion, by whatever means, is all that he can hope for.

For three ghastly days, Pete endures the presence of his mother. Eventually, he enters a weird world of his own, where he tries to blot out the horror of what is happening around him. And that is, perhaps, why he really has no idea of something that is happening right under his nose.

Others notice a softening in Dreadful Doris. Shipworms shudder to find that she is wearing more perfume than usual. A new tattoo appears on her brawny forearm. She wears her hat at a jaunty angle and her earrings become slightly less dangerous. And she takes to singing as she strolls. It's not a pleasant sound by any means, and the Killer Crabs all scuttle back to Canton as soon as she starts, but it is an improvement on the paint-stripping powers of her usual voice.

Pete, however, notices none of this. You can imagine the shock, then, when he enters the captain's cabin on the *Maiden's Rash* one day to find Dreadful Doris, his mother and tormentor, locked in a passionate embrace with . . .

Treacherous Trevor!

"Darling Petey-poops," yells Doris with a bashful smirk, "Trevor and I are going to tie the knot. Meet your new daddy!"

Pete's mind is unable to grasp this fresh awfulness. Does this mean . . . ? Will Trev and Doris live happily ever after here on the *Maiden's Rash?*

But Doris is still speaking. "I'm sorry, sweetie. Trev and I will be sailing off tomorrow on our honeymoon. Can you manage without your dear old mum?"

A joyous fact is bubbling up from Pete's boots and making its way to his brain. Doris is leaving. Trev is leaving. Together. For ever. Today!

For the first time in weeks, Pugnacious Pete smiles. "I'll try," he says.